Contents

fiction Green.

THE
SCARECROW

Brandon Robshaw

Published in association with
The Basic Skills Agency

Hodder & Stoughton
A MEMBER OF THE HODDER HEADLINE GROUP

Acknowledgements
Cover: Matthew Williams
Illustrations: Avril Turner

Orders: please contact Bookpoint Ltd, 130 Milton Park, Abingdon, Oxon OX14
4SB. Telephone: (44) 01235 827720, Fax: (44) 01235 400454. Lines are open from
9.00 - 6.00, Monday to Saturday, with a 24 hour message answering service.
Email address: orders@bookpoint.co.uk

British Library Cataloguing in Publication Data
A catalogue record for this book is available from The British Library

ISBN 0 340 84847 2

First published 2002
Impression number   10 9 8 7 6 5 4 3 2 1
Year   2005 2004 2003 2002

Typeset by SX Composing DTP, Rayleigh, Essex.
Printed in Great Britain for Hodder & Stoughton Educational, a division of
Hodder Headline Plc, 338 Euston Road, London NW1 3BH by Athenaeum
Press, Gateshead, Tyne & Wear.

1

A House in the Country

The big white house stood on a hill
in the middle of the fields.
Will stood on the steps
that led to the front door and looked around.
He could see for miles.
A patchwork of green and brown fields
as far as the eye could see.
Houses and farms were dotted
here and there.

'What do you think?' asked the estate agent.

'It's a fantastic view,' said Will.
'And I like the house.

How many bedrooms did you say
there are again?'

'Eight,' said the estate agent.
'And four reception rooms, a TV room,
a games room, a conservatory,
three bathrooms and a swimming pool.'

'Wow.'

'Yes, it's a very desirable property,'
said the estate agent.

'What are the neighbours like?' asked Will.
'All farmers, I suppose?'

'That's right.'
The estate agent pointed at
a grey stone building.
'That's Mr Sprott's farm.
He lives over there with his old mum.'

'What are they like?'
'Oh, they're nice enough people.
The old woman's a bit strange.
Some people say she's a witch!
She won't bother you, though.
They keep themselves to themselves.
All the fields over there belong to them.'

Sheep and cows stood in some of the fields.
Some were planted with crops.
A scarecrow stood in one of them.
Its arms were open wide.
It had a black hat on its head.

'That looks a bit creepy!' said Will.

'Oh, it's only a scarecrow.
Nothing to worry about.
What do you think?'

'I like it,' said Will.
'I like it a lot.
How much did you say?'

'£2 million pounds.'

'Right,' said Will.
'Cheque OK?'

2

A Rich Man

Will was a rich man.
He'd just won the lottery.
He couldn't believe it when he won.
He'd been doing it for years.
The same numbers every week.
He never really expected to win, though.
It was just a bit of fun.
He couldn't believe it
when his numbers came up.
He won £11 million.
It was a roll-over week.

He gave up his job as a postman.
Then he looked about
for a nice big house in the country.
He'd always wanted a house in the country.

And now he'd found one.
Will moved in straight away.
He drove there in his new Jaguar.
He ordered expensive furniture and carpets.
A king-size bed.
He had a jacuzzi put in.

He didn't give any money to charity.
Why should he?
It was his money.
He wasn't giving it to anyone else.

Will decided to hold a great big party.
He ordered 1000 bottles of wine.
Plenty of food.
A sound system and a top DJ from London.

He invited all his friends.
He didn't invite Mr Sprott
from the farm opposite.
He didn't invite any of his new neighbours.
Why should he?
They weren't his friends.
He didn't even know them.

The party started the Saturday
after Will moved in.
It was still going strong on Sunday night.

3

A Knock at the Door

Thud, thud, thud!
The noise of the drum and bass
thudded away.
It filled the whole house.
It echoed across the fields.

Some of Will's friends were still dancing.
Some had crashed out upstairs.
Will was in the jacuzzi, chilling out.
He was sharing a bottle of wine
with a beautiful blonde girl called Tina.

Then Will heard a sharp banging noise.

It was someone knocking at the front door.

'Who's that?' said Will.
'Why can't they leave us in peace?'

'Why doesn't someone else go?' said Tina.

'Oh, I'd better go.
You never know who it might be.
It could be trouble.'

Will got out of the jacuzzi
and went downstairs.
He opened the front door.
A large, red-faced man was standing there.
He wore a brown checked jacket
and a tweed cap.
He was holding a big stick.

'Who are you?' asked Will.
'What do you want?'

4
Jim Sprott

'I'm Jim Sprott
from across the way.
And I want you to turn
that bloody music off!
We can hear the noise right across the fields!'

'I'm having a party, all right?' said Will.
'If you don't like music, that's too bad.'

'But it's been going on for two days!
It's keeping my mother awake.
I'm asking you –
no, I'm telling you to turn it off!'

'Oh, are you?
Well, I'm not going to, mate.
This is my house
and I'll do what I like.'

'Turn it off!' shouted Jim Sprott.
He raised his stick suddenly.
'Turn it off, I tell you!'

Will took a step back.
'Watch what you're doing.
If you touch me with that stick
I'll have the police on you.'

Jim Sprott pushed his way into the house.
'Turn that bloody music off!'
'Get out of my house!' said Will.

'Not till you turn that bloody racket off!
Where's the music coming from?

If you don't turn it off
I'll smash the thing to pieces!'

Will stood in front of Jim Sprott.
'Just stop right there –'
Sprott raised his stick again
and hit Will on the arm.

'Ow!' said Will.
He snatched a wine bottle up from a table.
He smashed it over Sprott's head.

5

Dead!

_____

Jim Sprott grunted.
He put his hand to his head.
'Oh my Lord,' he said quietly.
Then he fell heavily to the floor.

Will bent down and touched Jim Sprott.
'Come on – you'll be all right . . .'

Mr Sprott didn't move.
He wasn't breathing.

Will ran and telephoned an ambulance.
They arrived within 20 minutes.
But Jim Sprott was dead on arrival
at the hospital.

6

The Trial

_____

There was a trial, of course.
Will was arrested and charged with murder.
He was kept in prison on remand
until his case came up.

Tina came to visit him in prison.
'Don't worry,' she said.
'You didn't mean to kill him, did you?
You'll get off.'

'I hope so,' said Will.

The day of the trial came at last.
Will was led into court
by two policemen.
He saw Tina standing there.
She smiled and waved.
Will tried to smile back.

Then he saw an old woman.
She looked at him with pure hate.
It gave Will quite a shock.
He wondered who she was.

Will was called to the stand.
His defence lawyer
asked him to say what had happened.
Will said he and Jim Sprott had argued.
Sprott had pushed into his house.
Sprott had hit him with a stick.
Will hit back with a bottle
in self-defence.
He didn't mean to kill Sprott.

Then the prosecuting lawyer came on.
He really went for Will.
He went over the story again and again,
trying to pick holes in it.
He tried to get Will to say
that he didn't get on with Sprott.
That he wanted to kill him.

Will stood firm.
He didn't mean to kill Sprott.
He killed him in self-defence.

When Will sat down,
he was soaked in sweat.
Tina smiled at him,
as if to say 'You did well.'

At the end, the judge asked the jury
to consider their verdict.
They were only gone a few minutes.

Then they came back.
Will held his breath
as he listened to the verdict.

'Not Guilty.'
It was a case of accidental death.
Will had killed Jim Sprott,
but only in self-defence.

Will sighed with relief.
Tina squeezed his hand.
They left the court still holding hands.

Outside, a woman stood in their way.
It was the old woman Will had seen in court.
She was still looking at him
with hate in her eyes.

'Excuse me,' said Will.

'No, I don't excuse you,' said the woman.
She was small, with long grey hair
'You killed my son.'

Will opened his mouth,
but couldn't find anything to say.

The old woman pointed
a skinny finger at Will.
'I curse you!
You'll die a violent death.
Just like my Jim did.
That's my curse.'

Will felt a chill run through him.
There was something scary
about the old woman.

Then she turned and shuffled away.
Will and Tina looked at each other,
speechless.

7

A Bad Shock

The next morning,
Will had a bad shock.
He was making coffee in the kitchen.
He looked out of the window
and saw Jim Sprott.
Sprott was standing in the field opposite.
He was wearing his brown checked jacket
and tweed cap.
His arms were spread wide.

Will's heart started pounding.
He stared at the figure,
waiting for it to move.

Nothing happened.
A minute went by.

Then Will suddenly got it.
It wasn't Jim Sprott at all.
It was the scarecrow.
That crazy old woman had put
Sprott's clothes on it.
Just to scare him.
Will laughed with relief.

He took some coffee up to Tina.
She had moved in with him now.
He told her about the scarecrow.
Tina shivered.

'I don't like that.
She's mad, that old woman.
What if she really is a witch?'

'Don't be silly,' said Will.
'She's just a crazy old girl.
She can't do anything –
except mess about dressing scarecrows up.'

'Maybe you should move away from here.
Sell the house and go.'
'Don't be silly!' said Will again.
'This is my house and I'm staying here.'

That night,
Will looked out of the window again.
He could just see
the figure of the scarecrow,
standing black against the starry sky.
It looked nearer than before.
But that must be his imagination.
Mustn't it?

8

A Bad Dream

_____

That night, Will had a bad dream.
He dreamed that the scarecrow
was climbing over the hedge.

It stumped up the path
on its broomstick legs.
It raised its broomstick arm.
It banged on the door . . .

Will woke up with a start.
His heart was beating fast.
He was covered in sweat.
What a terrible dream!

Then Will heard a noise.
A sharp, banging noise.
It was someone knocking at the front door.

Of course, thought Will.
He'd heard the knocking in his sleep.
That was why he'd dreamed that dream.

Tina was awake now.
'Who's that knocking at this time?'
The clock by the bed
showed that it was two o'clock
in the morning.
'Don't go.'

'Oh, I'd better go,' said Will.
'You never know who it might be.'

He got up and put on his
white silk dressing-gown.
He went to open the front door.

9

The Scarecrow

The scarecrow was standing there.
It was wearing Jim Sprott's
checked jacket and tweed cap.
It grinned at Will.

Will's heart thumped madly.
The old woman must have
brought the scarecrow here
and dumped it on his doorstep.
What an evil trick!
But he couldn't see anyone.
Just the scarecrow.

Then, it stepped forward
and pushed its way into the house.

Will backed away.

This can't be happening, he thought.

The scarecrow came towards him.

Will snatched up a wine bottle.

The scarecrow knocked the bottle

from his hand.

10

The End of Will

Tina lay in bed, scared.
She waited and waited,
but Will didn't come back.

At last, Tina reached for the telephone
by the bed.
She called the police.
They arrived within 20 minutes.
The front door was open.
Will was lying in the hall.
He was dead.
There were bits of straw scattered around.
A broken broomstick handle lay by the body.